DATE DUE

APR 7			
APR 7 1988			
DEC 0 8 1999			
AV JUL 2 2002			

The
Mind Angel
and Other Stories

The Lerner Science Fiction Library
Roger Elwood, Editor

The
Mind Angel
and Other Stories

Foreword by Isaac Asimov
Illustrations by Kathleen Groenjes

Lerner Publications Company
Minneapolis

International Standard Book Number: 0-8225-0958-X
Library of Congress Catalog Card Number: 73-21480

2   3   4   5   6   7   8   9   10   85   84   83   82   81   80   79   78   77

Contents

Foreword

Science fiction is about change. It is written because there *is* change in our world. In fact, all history is the story of how human life has changed, from the discovery of fire to the landing on the moon.

In ancient times, change was slow—so slow that no single person could see it taking place in his own lifetime. Changes did not often affect the lives of ordinary people. Kings came and went, armies won and lost, but life went on as usual.

When the age of modern science began, however, the rate of change increased, and people began to take notice. By the time the steam engine was invented toward the end of the 1700s, changes seemed to be taking place every day. Suddenly, there were steamships and railroads and telegraphs and sewing machines. The lives of ordinary people were no longer the same as the lives of their parents and grandparents.

Naturally, people began to wonder what further changes in living their children and grandchildren might experience. To satisfy their curiosity, they turned to science fiction. Science fiction writers speculated about the ways that life might change in the future. They invented new and different societies and told stories about them.

In the last few decades, change has become so rapid that our civilization and our very lives depend on our being able to understand and control change. It is as though we were in a racing automobile that we had to learn to steer in order to avoid a crash.

Science fiction can help us gain control of our future. It can help us understand the importance of change and the nature of the changes that may soon take place. In this way, science fiction gets us used to thinking in terms of the future. Because it is the only form of literature that does this, it plays a very important role in today's world.

Young people who grow up with science fiction have a real advantage. The training in imagination and forethought that they receive makes them better able to solve the problems we face now, and the still greater problems that we will face in coming years.

New York, New York
April, 1974   ISAAC ASIMOV

The
Mind Angel

"How do you like that father of mine?" Wanda asked. She was talking to Bruno—her alien pet, and her only real friend.

The star-shaped creature named Bruno seemed to float over the sand near the boots of Wanda's pressure suit. Suddenly, he sent a wave of love inside Wanda's mind, making her feel as if she were being hugged. This was Bruno's way of communicating with her.

After the feeling passed, Wanda stopped walking. She concentrated for a moment, organizing her thoughts, and then sent a wave of love back to Bruno. It was as if she were reaching down to cuddle him behind the neck.

"I wish I knew my father as well as I know you,"

Wanda said. She looked through her plexiglass helmet at the barren landscape of Armstrong's World, the third planet of the star Tau Ceti. Wanda and her pet were 12 light-years from Earth.

"Father doesn't understand *anything*," Wanda continued. "I've been cooped up in that stupid research station for five months now, and he hasn't let me see anything of this planet except a bunch of old pictures. He says it's 'too dangerous' for me to go off exploring by myself. Well, I'm out here now, and it doesn't look dangerous to me."

The skin of Bruno's body crinkled slightly, turning pale in the strong light of Armstrong's World.

Wanda frowned. "It's just like the time I found you on Mars," she complained. "After we made friends, Father wanted me to give you to the Museum of Alien Studies and let them put you in a cage, behind bars. He said it might be 'dangerous' for an Earth girl to have an alien pet. *Dangerous*, Bruno, imagine that! I knew he was wrong, but it took me almost forever to convince him. And it's all because he's so stubborn! If I hadn't disobeyed him and come out here on my own, I *never* would have gotten to see this planet, because Father *never* changes his mind. He's just too stubborn!"

It hurt Bruno to hear Wanda talk this way about her father. So after she had finished, he sent a strong, warm feeling into her mind. It was the same feeling Wanda experienced whenever her father looked into her eyes and hugged her because she had bruised her knee or stubbed her toe. He always hugged her until the pain went away, and Wanda loved him for it.

The feeling was hard to resist. But Wanda was still very angry, so she shook it away. Then she turned on Bruno. "Don't try that stuff on me!" she said sternly. "You always try to make me feel that way when you want me to stop doing or thinking something that hurts you. Well it isn't going to work this time, so you can just stop it!"

Trying to hide his feelings, Bruno pressed himself against the sand.

"Oh, Bruno," Wanda sighed. "I'm sorry I hurt you; I'll try not to do it again. It's just that Father is so unfair sometimes, and so stubborn. But I'll try to put all that out of my mind—I promise."

Before moving on, Wanda looked behind her. The research station was over the horizon—just out of sight—resting on a broad, level plain. Wanda turned back to Bruno. "Now that we're out here," she said, "we might as well enjoy ourselves."

She pressed a button on her pressure suit for a reading of her air supply. "I've got plenty of oxygen left," Wanda said. "And we've still got three hours

11

of light—enough to climb over those hills ahead of us and see what's on the other side. But we'd better hurry, Bruno. I'm due for a math lesson in a half-hour, and my father will probably send out a search party for me when he finds out that I've left the research station."

Wanda started to move forward. But Bruno hesitated, sending her a brief feeling of being left behind. When Wanda stopped and waited for him, Bruno lifted himself out of the sand. Then he began to float forward on his tiny feet.

Wanda began walking again. The hills seemed close, very close. But dressed in her bulky pressure suit, Wanda could not move more than a few yards a minute. Besides, Bruno kept lagging behind, forcing Wanda to wait for him. Wanda slowed her pace as she sent feelings of impatience back to her pet.

"Come on, Bruno!" she yelled. "You've got to move faster. There aren't that many hours of light left."

Bruno was 10 feet away from her. Suddenly, he began moving around in circles. Wanda strained her mind to pick up his feelings, but there was nothing.

"Bruno, don't play so hard to get," Wanda said softly. (Sometimes, Bruno played a game of keeping his thoughts to himself.) "If there's something the matter, let me know." She cleared her mind of thoughts and waited for some feelings from her pet. After a while, she realized that Bruno was staying silent longer than he ever had before.

Suddenly, a burst of pain entered Wanda's mind. She closed her eyes, and tears squeezed out of her eyelids, rolling down both cheeks. Forcing her eyes open, Wanda peered through the tears. Bruno was curled up on his back, his thousand tiny legs waving wildly.

Finally, the pain faded away. Moments later, Wanda felt something like a sigh pass through her mind. Bruno was still on his back, but his legs had stopped moving. Wanda moved to her pet's side, then lowered herself down on the knees of her pressure suit.

"Bruno!" she cried. "What's wrong!" There was no reply. Carefully, so as not to injure his tiny legs, Wanda cupped her gloves and lifted Bruno up. He was still breathing, still alive. But he did not move. Normally, his legs darted back and forth even while he slept; now, they were motionless. Wanda searched her mind for any feelings Bruno might be sending her. There was nothing. Not knowing what else to do, Wanda laid him back on the sand.

She waited. Ten minutes passed; then 20; then

40. Flipping a switch on her wrist, Wanda darkened her helmet's visor. Then she glanced up at Tau Ceti. The enormous star was close to the horizon now; less than an hour remained until sunset.

"I'll prove to my father that I can take care of myself," Wanda thought. First, she took care of Bruno. Whenever he was ready to sleep, he dug himself a shallow burrow in the sand. It was up to Wanda to do this now. Using a scoop from her suit's tool-pocket, she dug Bruno a hole. Then she picked him up and placed him in it. This done, she covered the hole with a thin plastic sheet; it would keep in the warmth throughout the cold night on Armstrong's World.

Having tended Bruno, Wanda began thinking about herself. There was nothing to worry about, she decided. She still had plenty of oxygen left, and her pressure suit was doing a good job of protecting her from the cold. She could stay with Bruno for at least another hour. Then, if he was still asleep, she could head back to the research station, leaving Bruno safe in his burro. "Yes," she thought, "and first thing tomorrow morning, I'll come back with a search party. Everything will turn out just fine."

Wanda was bending down to check Bruno when, out of the corner of her eye, she caught sight of a flashing pink light. Turning her head slightly, she saw a pink mist in the air, glowing from within. Slowly, the mist changed into the most beautiful woman Wanda had ever seen. Feathery white wings grew out of her back, and a halo of pink light glowed over her head. She was floating just a few feet off the ground.

Wanda wasn't sure, but she guessed that the beautiful woman was an angel. "Who are you?" she asked. "What do you want?"

"I am who you think I am, and I want only to help you." The angel's unspoken words oozed through Wanda's mind like honey dripping down into a bowl. "This planet is a dusty wasteland, with air so thin that nothing can grow. How can you mortals live here? Wouldn't you like to see LIFE growing out of these rocks?"

The angel moved her arms up in a sweeping motion. "First, we need some trees!"

All at once, Armstrong's World began to change. Large trees with orange branches pushed themselves up out of the sand. Their trunks were huge, with bark that thickened even as Wanda watched. The trees grew higher, and roots sprang out of the ground, traveling over the surface for yards—half in, and half out, of the soil. Branches crisscrossed the air, forming a canopy over Wanda's head. And still, the trees grew higher.

The angel looked pleased. "Now let the weeds grow!" she commanded.

With this, the trees suddenly stopped growing. Then vines and weeds began to grow at their bases.

"I almost forgot the flowers!"

Blossoms sprouted everywhere, growing from stems that sprang up from the ground and out of the tree trunks. Wanda had never seen so many plants before! These growths were shaped like the green plants of Earth, but they were in totally different colors. The leaves were red and orange, and the flowers were streaked with pinks and yellows, browns and blues.

Wanda was now standing in the middle of a lush jungle-paradise. Huge purple clouds passed overhead, and just below them, strange birds with rainbow-colored feathers flapped their wings. As Wanda watched the birds descend from flight, it began to rain. The life-giving rainwater flowed into shimmering pools, and silver fish leaped out of them, snapping at insects that buzzed over the surface. After the rain stopped, a thick gray mist hovered over the jungle floor, slowly rising to the tops of the trees. Then a flood of sunshine burst through the mist and dried up all the water. Her eyes aglow, Wanda could only marvel at the powers of the beautiful angel now floating above her head.

The angel smiled. "Wanda, there's AIR outside your helmet now! Look—fresh, clean air!" The angel did not move her lips, but Wanda heard her clearly.

"The air carries the sweetest smells in the universe, Wanda. Your pressure suit is a prison! Your kind wasn't meant to be cooped up in tubes and wires, breathing stale air."

Wanda heard the hiss of air inside her suit. It smelled rotten, as if it had been breathed by a thousand lungs. How wonderful it would be to cast off her suit and step out into the sweet-smelling flowers, Wanda thought. But would it be safe? Was there *really* air out there?

The angel floated closer to her. "You're a sweet girl, Wanda, an intelligent girl. Your gentle hands would shelter any flower they touched. Step out of your suit, Wanda! Breathe the fresh air; smell the fragrant flowers."

"I want to," Wanda said, "but . . . "

"I know what you're thinking, Wanda; I read the fears in your mind. You're *afraid*—afraid there might not really be any air out here. But, Wanda, I just told you that there is! Do you think I would lie to you or try to hurt you?"

"No," Wanda answered, "I don't think that. But something is stopping me. Another voice is trying to reach me; it's trying to warn me of something — something dangerous."

"Ignore the other voice, Wanda! It is evil. Open your mind to me, and erase all your other thoughts. NOTHING can harm you, Wanda, for you are not like other mortals. An ordinary person would die instantly out here without a mask. But you are *special*, Wanda, special! You could take off your suit and be perfectly safe out here, among the trees and flowers. Nothing can harm you."

The other voice was gone now, and Wanda was no longer afraid. Staring into the angel's eyes, she felt stronger than she had ever felt before. "I AM special!" she thought. "Nothing can harm me!"

The angel moved even closer now. "STEP OUT OF YOUR SUIT, WANDA! Set yourself free, and grow wings like mine. Then you can fly, Wanda, to places in the clouds beyond your wildest dreams."

It would be easy, Wanda decided. There were only two catches on her helmet, and all she had to do was open them. Then she could be free.

"Go ahead, Wanda! Open the catches and let the helmet slip off."

As if in a trance, Wanda flipped open the first catch. A split second later, a red light blinked on inside her helmet, warning that only one small catch separated her from the atmosphere of Armstrong's World. But Wanda had nothing to worry about; she was special.

Her eyes on the angel, Wanda brought up her glove to the second catch. But just as she was about to open it—her hand froze! She couldn't move it at all! Her mind grew muddled, confused. Wanda was hearing *two* voices now: the angel's, and the other one, the one she had heard before. As the voices struggled for control, Wanda noticed that the angel seemed to be fading back into the mist. At the same time, Wanda was becoming aware of another presence; it was growing stronger, Stronger, STRONGER.

"BRUNO!" Wanda screamed, seeing her pet come toward her. "Bruno!" Suddenly, the angel dissolved back into the mist and disappeared. Then the trees disappeared, and the weeds, and the flowers. *Everything* was gone now!

"What am I doing!" Wanda cried, flipping the first catch back on. "Oh, Bruno, it was *your voice* I heard before! You were trying to warn me about her. But I couldn't think straight."

Bruno sent a feeling of hope into Wanda's mind. Then, without warning, he ran away from her on his tiny legs, back toward the research station.

"Don't leave me here!" Wanda shouted. Looking toward the horizon, she saw a light flickering in the distance. Bruno was heading straight for it.

"A search party," Wanda thought, switching on her shortwave radio. "Wanda Johnson calling!" she cried into the microphone. *"Help! Help!"*

A light flashed behind her. Wanda turned and saw the pink mist floating above the ground. In a matter of seconds, the mist changed back into the angel. She looked angry now, and not nearly so beautiful as before. "Your pet is evil, Wanda!" came her voice. "It kept me from talking to you by sending *pain* into my mind!"

Wanda tried to ignore the angel's words. "Help!" she sobbed into the radio. "Hurry! Please!"

"Sleep, Wanda, sleep," the angel's voice chanted in her head. Wanda kept trying to call for help, but something stopped her mouth and tongue from moving. "Listen only to my voice, Wanda. *Sleep. Sleep.*"

Wanda felt her eyelids grow heavy, but she forced herself to keep them half open. Then she looked in the direction that Bruno had gone. The flashing light on the horizon was brighter now; the search party must have heard her pleas for help.

"You can't make me do anything I don't want to do!" Wanda shouted at the angel.

"Sleep, Wanda, *sleep."*

"I won't!" Wanda screamed. "I won't!"

21

The angel shimmered, as if about to fade back into the pink mist. Then something stirred up the dust from the ground, making the mist swirl around in great clouds. A glove suddenly emerged from the clouds. It grabbed the shoulder of Wanda's suit. "Wanda!" came her father's voice. "Are you all right?"

"Father! Watch out for it!"

All at once, the clouds disappeared. The pink mist was gone now, and no trace of the angel remained. Wanda's father looked down at her, a pistol-like object in his hand. "Wanda," he said, "the thing you saw won't come back. I used this gun to set up an electromagnetic force field; it drove the thing away."

"But, Father—what was it?"

"We're not sure, Wanda, but we think it's a form of life native to Armstrong's World. It seems to be able to change its form at will. By some kind of telepathic power, it forces itself inside the human mind. It's invisible most of the time, and impossible to detect. That's why I told you never to leave the research station, Wanda. And that's why no one but the geology research team is allowed out on the surface."

Wanda looked up and saw a scout craft hovering about 50 feet above her. It landed slowly, its retrorockets firing. "I'm sorry I caused so much trouble," Wanda said. "But I felt so cooped up in the research station, and I didn't really think it would be dangerous out here."

"Well, Wanda, I guess you know better now."

"Oh, yes, Father. It was terrible! I was just standing here, waiting for Bruno to wake up, when this beautiful angel came out of the clouds. But it was really a *devil*, Father, and it tried to make me kill myself! It told me to take off my pressure suit and breathe the air!"

"Yes, Wanda, I believe you. You see, the angel that appeared to you is a telepathic creature. It can read memories, and it can make itself look like things anyone can recognize. Once it gets inside a person's mind, anything can happen. Judging from the telepathic message Bruno sent me, I'd say this mind angel must have given you a pretty bad scare."

Wanda had almost forgotten about Bruno. Now, as she stepped aboard the scout craft, she became aware of his presence. He was inside the ship, sending her feelings of warmth and relief. After Wanda spotted Bruno, she ran over and picked him up. Then she looked out the window as the ship lifted off. Below her, there was nothing but an endless stretch of sand.

"I'll never go out there alone again, Father," Wanda promised. "But I'd sure like to find out what makes these creatures tick."

"I was afraid of that!" her father laughed. "Once a scientist's daughter, always a scientist's daughter. I guess your curiosity just can't be dampened. Well, it just so happens that there's an expedition in the works to discover exactly what these creatures are. As the beginning of your scientific education—and as punishment for your stunt today—YOU'LL handle all the paper work!"

Wanda winced, then turned to Bruno and smiled. Inside, she was glad; the punishment could have been much worse. And besides, her father hadn't said anything about grounding her!

Keeping her thoughts to herself, Wanda again fixed her eyes on the surface of Armstrong's World. Soon, she would be back down there, joining the search for the mind angel—a demon in disguise. Her father would be sure to let her go, Wanda decided. After all, she and Bruno had a score to settle!

The
Green Boy

It was a warm autumn day, and golden leaves fell to the ground from sunlit trees. As Timmy Jackson walked along the woodland path behind his house, he slapped a tree branch against his leg. Timmy liked the woods. He liked the stillness that surrounded the trees, and he liked to sit beside the brook and listen to the water flowing over the rocks.

As Timmy neared the brook, the stillness of the woods was suddenly broken by a strange, haunting sound. Alarmed, Timmy stopped, then cocked his ears and listened. Soon, he heard some heartbreaking sobs coming through the trees in front of him. Someone was crying, he thought.

Timmy raced down the path until he came to a clearing. Then, to his wide-eyed amazement, he spied a little green boy. The boy was sitting on a tree stump, rubbing his eyes with his fingers as a stream of green tears rolled down his cheeks. He wore green boots, green pants, and a green shirt with a strange emblem on it. And—as if this weren't enough—even his *hair*, *face*, and *fingers* were green! Timmy could hardly believe it.

When the boy looked up and saw Timmy, his green eyes filled with fear. Then, as Timmy approached him, the little green boy stood up. The two boys were relieved when they saw they were the same height, yet both of them were trembling.

"Who . . . are you?" asked Timmy, in a quivery voice.

"My name is Hue," replied the little green boy, his voice also quivering.

"Where did you come from?"

The green boy pointed his finger up to the sky. "From up there," he said.

"What do you mean?" asked Timmy, his blue eyes squinting at the afternoon sun.

"I came here with my mother and father in a flying saucer," the green boy said. He pointed across the clearing to a large circle of scorched leaves. "We landed right over there."

When Timmy saw the landing spot, his eyes became as big as balloons. He thought of all the exciting stories he'd read about flying saucers and visitors from other planets. "Gee whiz!" he cried. "You mean, you came from *Mars?*"

Timmy's friendliness put Hue at ease, and his little green tears finally stopped. "I come from the planet Anamoss," he said, his voice calm now, but serious. "There's a war going on there. We're fighting the pink people."

"The pink people?" Timmy asked.

"Yes. Either they or we will win control of the planet. My parents are hiding me here on Earth until the war is over." From the back pocket of his green pants, he took out a small bottle filled with pellets as tiny as BBs. "They left me with enough food to last a very long time."

Timmy stared wide-eyed at the bottle. "That green stuff is *food?*" he said. "Gee whiz!"

They sat down together on the tree stump, and the green boy told Timmy about the planet he'd come from. Hue explained that the green people and the pink people had started fighting because they each wanted to control the planet. "My father thinks the war will last at least a hundred years," he said.

"A hundred years!" yelled Timmy. "But that's forever!"

"No," the green boy corrected him. "A hundred

years isn't long at all, not by our time. I myself am already eleven hundred years old! You see, a hundred years of our time is equal to only one year of your time."

Timmy nodded, his eyes alive and dancing. "Tell me more about your planet, Hue," he pleaded.

The green boy told Timmy many strange things about the place he had come from. "Anamoss resembles Earth," he said, "except that all the birds there fly upside down. And all the dogs have six legs. And all the cats croak like frogs. And all—"

"Anamoss sure sounds like a strange place," interrupted Timmy.

"Anamoss is a *beautiful* place!" said Hue. "It has light-blue grass, and a rainbow-colored sky. And when it snows, the flakes are soft and warm — and green. Pink popsicle trees grow out of the rocks, and golden water flows through all the rivers and streams."

Timmy's jaw fell open. "Golden water!" he cried. "And pink popsicle trees! And — and GREEN snow!"

As Hue went on to describe how happy the green and pink people had been before they went to war with each other, he again became sad and gloomy. "Everyone is fighting now," he sobbed, "and the rivers are filled with blood. Oh, I just hope the war ends soon, so my parents can come back and get me."

"Where are you going to stay while you're on Earth?" Timmy asked.

"I'll wait right here," the green boy replied. "In the woods."

"But you can't stay here for a whole year! Where will you sleep?"

"We don't sleep on Anamoss," Hue said. "We stay awake all the time."

Timmy's jaw fell open again. Then he said: "But you can't stay in the woods *all alone*, Hue. Come home with me! Please!"

After hesitating, the green boy agreed to go home with Timmy. As they started walking up the path to Timmy's house, Timmy noticed a little red light bulb attached to Hue's belt buckle. "What's the red light for, Hue?" he asked.

"It's a signal light," Hue explained. "When my mother and father come back to get me, it will start flashing."

When the two boys got to Timmy's house, they opened the back door and stepped into the kitchen. Timmy's mother was washing dishes at the sink. "Hey, Mom!" Timmy shouted. "Look!"

Timmy's mother did just that, staring unbelievingly at Hue for what seemed like hours. "Why, he's GREEN!" she finally exclaimed. "A little green boy! And so cute!"

Within an hour, the whole town of Northwind knew of Timmy's amazing discovery. The first person to arrive at Timmy's house was the governor, who spent over 45 minutes viewing and interviewing the green boy. A while later, a group of FBI agents arrived from Washington. Hue agreed to answer their questions. But first, he made them promise to let him stay at Timmy's house until his parents came back from Anamoss to get him. After the FBI agents agreed to this, Hue told them all they wanted to know. They were especially interested in the war between the green people and the pink people for the control of Anamoss, and they asked Hue many questions about it. Finally, after all their questions had been answered, they went away, leaving the green boy in the hands of Timmy's parents.

After the excitement of Hue's arrival died down, Hue and Timmy got to know each other better. They played together constantly as the days passed into weeks, and the weeks passed into months. Flocks of curious sightseers still came to Northwind to see the little green boy, but they were stopped at the town's borders by state police.

Every night, Timmy would lie in his bed and look

at Hue, who always stood his sleepless vigil at the bedroom window, looking up at the distant stars. One night when Timmy couldn't sleep, the little green boy sat down on Timmy's bed, and the two boys talked. "Hue, do you miss your mother and father very much?" Timmy asked.

"Yes," the green boy replied.

"Gee, Hue. Aren't you happy here at all?"

"I like you and your parents very much, Timmy. But I miss my home, and I want to return to it." Too unhappy to say anything else, Hue left Timmy and walked back to the window. With sad green eyes, he looked back up at the faraway stars.

The next morning, right after the two boys had eaten breakfast, Timmy's mother called Timmy into the living room. She sensed that he was upset, and she wanted to talk with him. "Timmy," she said quietly, "I know you've grown fond of Hue. Your father and I have, too. But one day, Hue will be leaving us. Just keep remembering this, dear, so that when the time comes for him to go, you'll be expecting it, and you won't feel too bad."

"Okay, Mom," Timmy said sadly. "I'll remember." His head hung low, Timmy walked back into the kitchen. Then he looked out the kitchen window and saw Hue playing in the backyard. The little green boy was swinging back and forth on the tire that Timmy's father had tied to the tree branch. "I know Hue wants to go home," thought Timmy, "but I'm sure going to miss him. He's just about the best friend I've ever had."

Every night now, Timmy watched Hue become sadder and sadder as the green boy waited at the bedroom window for his parents to arrive. And every day, Timmy kept glancing at the little red light bulb on Hue's belt buckle, waiting for it to start flashing, but hoping in his heart that it never would . . .

. . . It was late autumn already, and the ground was again covered with golden leaves. Timmy and Hue were helping Timmy's parents rake the backyard when suddenly, it happened! The red light on Hue's belt buckle began flashing on and off, going BLEEP-BLEEP, BLEEP-BLEEP, BLEEP-BLEEP. Not sure whether he was sad or happy — or *both* — Timmy turned to the green boy and just looked at him for a moment. "Oh, Hue!" he finally said. "Your parents have come for you!"

The green boy shook hands with Timmy's father and hugged Timmy's mother goodbye. "I'll always remember you," he told them. "You're my second parents." Then Hue and Timmy started walking into the woods. When they came to the spot where

Timmy had first met the green boy, they found Hue's mother and father waiting there, standing beside a green flying saucer.

"Hue, darling!" the green boy's mother cried, as she swept him into her arms and hugged him. "Oh, how I've missed you!" After getting another big hug from his father, Hue introduced Timmy to his parents. Timmy liked them right away. They were green, like Hue, and every bit as nice.

"I have some good news for you, Son," Hue's father said. "The war on Anamoss is finally over. The green people and the pink people have realized that fighting each other will never bring happiness, and they have agreed to live together in peace and brotherhood."

"That's wonderful news, Father," said Hue. "I'm glad the war's over, and glad we're together again. But, to be honest, I'm also sad, because I'll have to leave Timmy now." As Hue shook Timmy's hand and said goodbye, two green tears rolled down his cheeks. "I'll come back and visit you, Timmy," he said. "I promise! Well—so long."

Hue's father put his green hands on Timmy's shoulders. "You'd better leave now, Timmy," he said softly. "We'll be taking off soon, and the noise might hurt your ears."

Timmy waved goodbye to Hue and his parents,

then turned around and started walking back home. Minutes later, he heard a loud humming sound. He turned around quickly, but he was too late; the flying saucer had already risen up through the trees and out of sight.

When Timmy got back home, he began telling his parents all about the green flying saucer, and about Hue's mother and father. Suddenly, his eyes caught sight of something. He ran to the kitchen window and pointed up to the sky. "Mom! Dad!" he shouted. "Look! Up there!"

Together, Timmy and his parents saw the green flying saucer swoop straight down to them from a cloud. Then—as the saucer slowly circled the top of their house—they saw Hue! He was waving goodbye to them from inside the saucer's large round window. The saucer circled the house three times, then flew straight back up and disappeared into the afternoon sky.

"Have a good trip!" Timmy shouted after his friend. "And don't forget your promise. Because if I have to, I'll wait for you until OUR snow turns green—and that's a promise!"

E. Michael Blake

The
Translator

It was a hot, bright day—perfect for swimming or softball. Nearly all the days were perfect here, in the Korr Highlands on the planet Sarayn. But 10-year-old Terri Wolenski wasn't happy. She didn't feel like swimming today, and there was no one to play softball with. No one, for Terri Wolenski was the only human child on the entire planet.

After building a castle on the sandy beach, Terri headed back to the shelter. There was no other place to go. As she wandered along, she complained to herself about being stuck on the alien planet. "This place isn't any fun," she thought for the millionth time. "No other kids around. And I *still* have to go to school!"

Terri was tutored by her mother every morning. During the evenings, her mother helped Terri's father with his research. Terri's father was involved in something called "interplanetary communication," and he was studying the languages spoken by the intelligent creatures of Sarayn.

As Terri approached the shelter—a group of connected plastic domes—her father stepped outside, grinning. "Terri!" he called out. "Come in and see the translator. I've finished it!"

She followed him in, not very excited. "Daddy's worked so hard on that machine," Terri thought, "and all he can do with it is talk to those strange little furries."

Terri and her father went through the living-room dome, into a plastic hallway, and then into the laboratory. There, along with all the tables full of electrical equipment and research notes, was a native Saraynian—or a "furry."

"Here's the translator," said Terri's father, holding up a small metal box in the palm of his hand. "With this, I can talk to Beydaf, here, without trying to speak his language."

Terri didn't want to be rude, but she couldn't help staring at the Saraynian. Like all furries, Beydaf was short (about four feet high), mostly round (like a tire), and covered all over with thick yellow fur. He had no legs, but he had four brown tentacles for arms, and two pair of eyes on either side of his body. To Terry, Saraynians were strange

—too strange to be pets. But they were supposed to be very friendly, and, in their own way, they were as intelligent as human beings.

Eager to demonstrate his invention, Terri's father spoke through a small grille in the translator. "Beydaf," he said, "I'd like you to meet my daughter. Her name is Terri." Dr. Wolenski pressed a button, and a shrill whistle came out of the translator. It sounded like the "voices" that Terri had heard in the Saraynians' village.

Beydaf whistled back a reply. Then Terri's father pressed another button on the translator, and a humanlike voice spoke from it. "I greet you, Terri, and I wish you well. Dr. Wolenski, your device works quite well. I understand you perfectly."

Terri smiled politely. She wasn't really interested.

"Terri," her father said, holding out the translator, "this is yours."

Her eyes widened. "Mine? But why?"

Dr. Wolenski smiled. "I know you've been lonely, with no kids here. But with the translator, you can talk to Saraynians. And there are plenty of Saraynian children in Beydaf's village."

Terri frowned. "Why would I want to talk to them?"

"Well, Saraynian children aren't all that different from human children. They grow up at about the same rate, and they like to play games and have fun."

Terri glanced at the furry. She didn't think something like *that* could play tag or softball.

"Now, Terri," her father said, "there are some things you will have to learn about the translator. Just because you can talk to Saraynians with it doesn't mean that you can say just anything that pops into your head."

"I'll be polite," Terri said.

"That's not what I mean," her father chuckled. "I know you'll be polite. What I'm getting at is that there are some words in our language that simply won't translate into theirs, even with the translator."

"Why?"

"Well, a language is a way of telling someone about something. If you lived in a world like this one, where the natives had never even *seen* a machine until we landed here, you wouldn't have any words for machines in your language. Someone has to think of something, and then invent words to explain it to someone else."

"I don't understand," Terri said, shaking her head in confusion.

"Well, if you had never seen or heard about a spaceship, would you know what powered it? Could you think of words to describe it? No, of course not. And it's the same with the Saraynians.

I could say 'nuclear reaction motor' to Beydaf, through the translator, all day long—and he still wouldn't understand me, because the Saraynians don't have any words for 'nuclear reaction motor' in their language."

"So how do I use the translator?" Terri asked.

"By stopping to think before you talk, and by choosing your words carefully."

Beydaf tapped Terri's father on the arm with a tentacle. Seeing him, Dr. Wolenski pushed a button on the translator. "Yes, Beydaf?" he said, and then pressed the other button.

"Excuse me, Dr. Wolenski," the translator spoke after Beydaf's whistling, "but I must return to my village now. Thank you for having me as your guest, and for letting me use your wonderful translator."

"You're quite welcome," Terri's father returned. "I'll let you know when I've built more translators, so you can give some to the villagers."

"Thank you," replied Beydaf. As Terri watched, Beydaf's fur began bristling. Then his round body lifted slightly off the floor, and he coasted out of the laboratory.

Terri stared after him, though she had seen Saraynians "coasting" many times before. "How do they do that?" she asked her father.

"They ride the currents of the planet's magnetic field to create a rotary force that lets them move in any direction on the surface," he answered.

Terri shook her head again.

"Sorry," Dr. Wolenski chuckled. "I'm getting too technical. It's like this. Saraynians have a special organ in their bodies that uses magnetism to skim above the surface, the way we use legs to push us along the ground."

"Why don't they have legs?" she asked.

"Terri," her father replied, putting a hand on her shoulder, "why don't WE coast on magnetism? It has to do with evolution and natural selection. It's very complicated, and we may never discover all the answers. This is a whole new world we're studying, Terri—I've only translated the language of the Korr Highlands. All of the things here—the plants, animals, soil, air, oceans—are completely different from Earth's. And we don't even know all about Earth yet!"

Terri still didn't understand, but she wasn't interested enough to ask any more questions.

"Anyway," her father said, "the translator is all yours. Why don't you head over to the Saraynian village and try it out?"

"I might," Terri said, taking the translator. She was afraid her father would be disappointed because of her indifference, but his expression didn't seem to change as she walked out of the lab, translator in hand.

Terri wandered outside the shelter for a long time, looking down at the translator occasionally, and pouting to herself. "Who needs this dopey thing?" she thought. "I don't want to talk to *furries*. They're nothing like real kids."

She walked on aimlessly, fingering the little metal box all the while. Even though it could be held in one hand, the translator contained an extremely complicated computer. In it were stored all the sounds and words of both English and the language of the Korr Highlands. When a Saraynian word entered the translator's built-in microphone, the computer decoded it, computed the English version of the word, and then "voiced" the translated word over a small speaker. English words were translated into the language of the Korr Highlands in the same way, making the translator a truly remarkable device. To Terri Wolenski, however, it was nothing more than a "dopey thing."

Suddenly, a BOOM! thundered at Terri, nearly knocking her down on the shaking ground. The explosion was so loud that it hurt her head. Terri whirled around to see what had happened, but she saw only miles and miles of hills and grasslands.

It was then that she realized how far she had wandered—the shelter wasn't anywhere in sight.

Then Terri heard a loud crackling sound. It was coming from behind a hill thick with stubby blue trees. Slowly, she climbed the hill, trying to be brave but ready to turn around and run if she had to.

When she reached the top of the hill, Terri saw bright yellow flames jumping out of a field full of charred metal. She suddenly recognized the place as the fuel yard, where their spaceship and extra fuel was kept. And down there, almost trapped in the fire, was a small Saraynian!

Almost without thinking, Terri pressed a button on the translator and yelled, "What are you doing down there?" She pressed the other button and heard the translator say, "I was just playing! Please help me, whoever you are!"

"What's wrong with you?" Terri yelled back, watching a sea of flames approach the unmoving Saraynian. "Don't you see how close the fire is to you?"

"No! I can't see *anything*! The fire blinded me!" came the answer.

"Run!" Terri yelled, barely remembering to keep switching the buttons. "Run, run!"

"What?" the translator said. "I don't understand. What are you saying?"

"I said RUN! The fire is closing in on you!"

"I know that, but what is this 'run' you're talking about?"

"The translator isn't working," Terri thought. "It's not telling him to run." Then, all at once, she realized what the problem was: the furry *couldn't* run because he had no legs! And he didn't understand what "run" meant because there was no word for "run" in his language.

Carefully, Terri tried again. "Lift yourself off the ground."

The Saraynian bristled his fur and rose. "You mean there's a way out?"

"Yes!" yelled Terri. "Go backward—slowly."

The little furry backed up, edging away from the nearest wall of flames. By now, robots from the spaceship were starting to put out the fire. But none of them was close enough to save the Saraynian.

"Now go left a little," Terri said, steering the furry away from another blaze.

Just then, one of the robots veered in between the Saraynian and the fire, putting the flames out with an extinguisher. The furry was safe at last!

"Am I out yet?"

"Yes, yes!" answered Terri. "Just wait there, and I'll get help!"

Terri turned and ran down the hill, back toward

the shelter. She raced all the way home, into the laboratory, and into her father's arms. Breathless and crying, she told her father about the fire, and about how the furry had almost died in it.

❖ ❖ ❖ ❖

"I acted like a big baby yesterday," Terri thought to herself. "I shouldn't have cried, even if I was scared."

But Terri was the only one who seemed concerned about her crying. Her parents were very proud of her. And so were Beydaf and Duzo, the young Saraynian she had rescued from the fire.

"Duzo, here, didn't know what was in your storage yard," Beydaf said through the translator. "He played with the knobs on one of the fuel containers, until it began hissing. Luckily, he coasted far enough away to escape the explosion. I apologize for your loss of flying fluid."

"No problem," Terri's father said. "We have another yard with emergency fuel. Anyway, I'm glad Terri learned how to use the translator."

"So am I!" said Duzo. "And all the time, I thought it was someone from my village who was talking to me. I couldn't have made it without you, Terri Wolenski."

"Gee," Terri said, looking at Duzo. Hearing the

furry's words in English made the creature seem less strange, somehow—almost like a person.

"Would you like to come to the village with me?" Duzo went on. "I can see again now, and you can come play with me and the other kids."

"Why don't you, Terri?" her mother said, smiling.

"But, what could we play?" Terri asked. "I'm so different from them."

"Terri," her father said, mussing her hair, "if you could figure out how to talk to them, all by yourself, you could do *anything* with them."

"I could?" she asked.

"Yes. Believe me."

Still a little confused, Terri left with Beydaf and Duzo. She spent the rest of the day in the Saraynian village, meeting the kids. And her father was right: she really *could* play with them. In fact, she'd never had so much fun playing tag in her life!

The Lerner Science Fiction Library

Night of the Sphinx and Other Stories
Adrift in Space and Other Stories
The Killer Plants and Other Stories
The Tunnel and Other Stories
Journey to Another Star and Other Stories
The Missing World and Other Stories
The Graduated Robot and Other Stories
The Mind Angel and Other Stories

We specialize in publishing quality books for
young people. For a complete list please write:

LERNER PUBLICATIONS COMPANY
241 First Avenue North, Minneapolis, Minnesota 55401